Five Little Fiends

For my mum and my dad
and my brother, Stew

Copyright © 2001 by Sarah Dyer
With many thanks to the BA Illustration Department, Kingston

First U.S. Edition 2002
Published by Bloomsbury, New York and London
Distributed to the trade by St. Martin's Press
Library of Congress Cataloging-in-Publication Data
Dyer, Sarah, 1978-
Five little fiends / Sarah Dyer.
p.cm Summary: Five little fiends steal pieces of the world to admire, but give
them back when they realize the beauty comes from being connected.
ISBN 1-58234-751-4 (alk. paper)
[1. Monsters—Fiction. 2. Whole and parts (Philosophy)—Fiction. 3. Sharing—Fiction. 4. Earth—Fiction.]
I. Title.   PZ27.D9884 Fi 2002   [E]—dc21
2001043906
Printed in Belgium
1 3 5 7 9 10 8 6 4 2

Bloomsbury USA Children's Books
175 Fifth Avenue
New York, New York 10010

FIVE LITTLE FIENDS

SARAh DYeR

BLOOMSBURY
CHILDREN'S
BOOKS

On a faraway plain stood five lonely statues.

Inside each statue
lived a little fiend.

Every day they would come outside
to marvel at their surroundings.

One
day
they
each
decided
to
take
the
one
thing
they
liked
best.

One took the sun,

one took the land,

one took the sky,

one took the sea,

one took the moon.

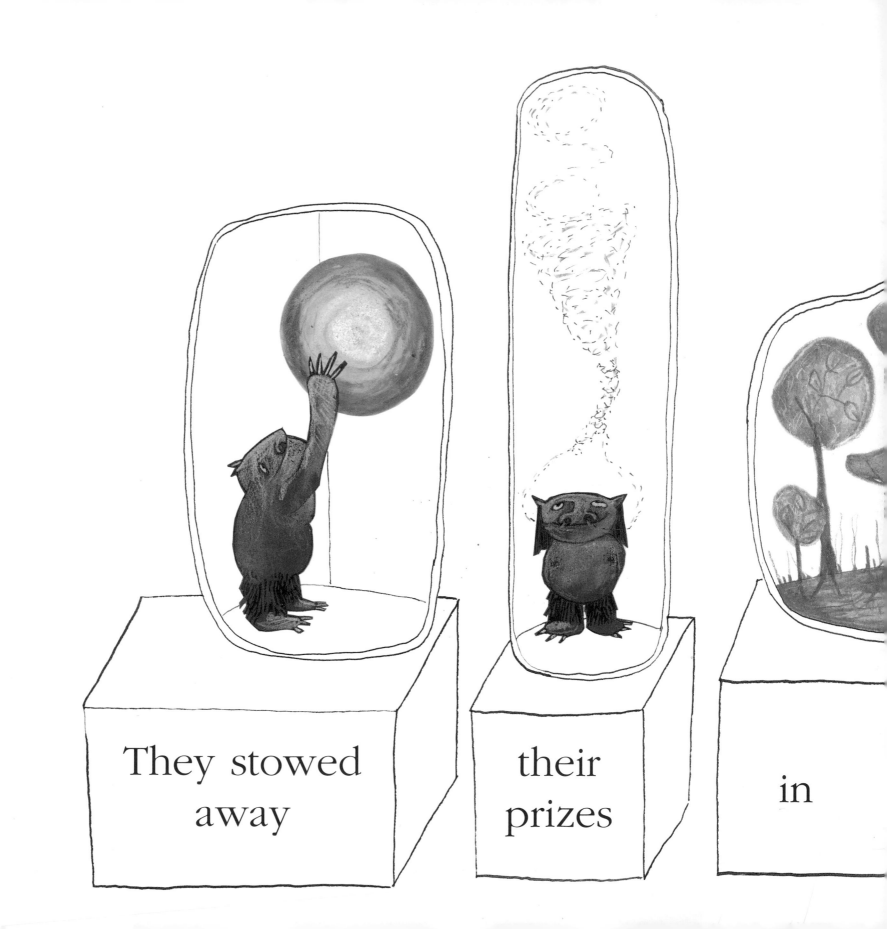

They stowed away

their prizes

in

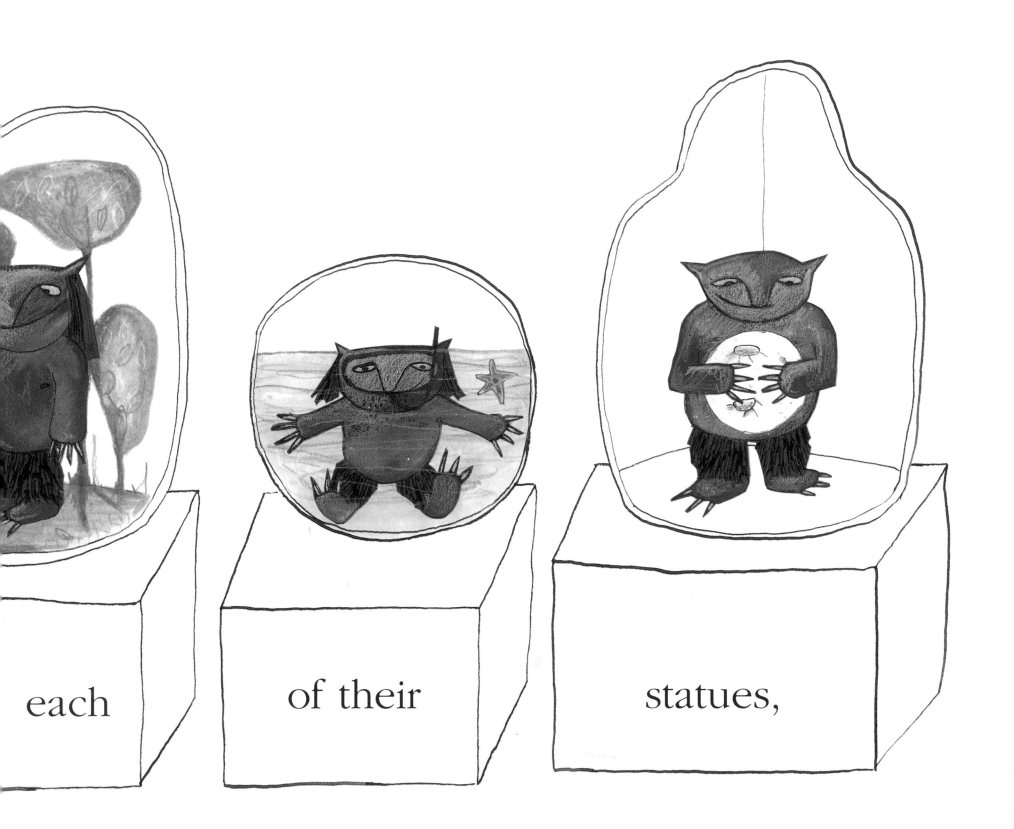

each   of their   statues,

and admired them.

But they soon realized that . . .

. . . the sun could not stay up without the sky,

the
sky
was
nowhere
to
be
found
without
the
land,

the land started to die
without water from the sea,

the sea could not flow
without the pull of the moon,

and the moon could not glow
without the light from the sun.

So they decided . . .

. . . to put everything back,

and once again marvel at their surroundings.